Dear Parents and Educators,

Welcome to Penguin Young Readers! As parents and educators, you know that each child develops at his or her own pace—in terms of speech, critical thinking, and, of course, reading. Penguin Young Readers recognizes this fact. As a result, each Penguin Young Readers book is assigned a traditional easy-to-read level (1–4) as well as a Guided Reading Level (A–P). Both of these systems will help you choose the right book for your child. Please refer to the back of each book for specific leveling information. Penguin Young Readers features esteemed authors and illustrators, stories about favorite characters, fascinating nonfiction, and more!

Kate & Mim-Mim: Kate's Wish

LEVEL **3**

GUIDED READING LEVEL **J**

This book is perfect for a **Transitional Reader** who:
- can read multisyllable and compound words;
- can read words with prefixes and suffixes;
- is able to identify story elements (beginning, middle, end, plot, setting, characters, problem, solution); and
- can understand different points of view

Here are some **activities** you can do during and after reading this book:
- Story Map: A story map is a visual organizer that helps explain what happens in a story. On a separate piece of paper, create a story map of this story. The map should include the beginning (who are the characters and what will they be doing?), the middle (what are the characters doing after the story gets started?), and the ending (how does the story end?).
- Character Traits: In the story, Mim-Mim describes himself as "clumsy." Come up with a list of other words to describe him.

Remember, sharing the love of reading with a child is the best gift you can give!

—Sarah Fabiny, Editorial Director
   Penguin Young Readers program

*Penguin Young Readers are leveled by independent reviewers applying the standards developed by Irene Fountas and Gay Su Pinnell in *Matching Books to Readers: Using Leveled Books in Guided Reading*, Heinemann, 1999.

PENGUIN YOUNG READERS
An Imprint of Penguin Random House LLC

© 2013 KMM Productions Inc. a Nerd Corps company. Licensed by FremantleMedia Kids & Family Entertainment. Based on the episode "Teenie Genie" written by Julie & Scott Stewart. Published in 2016 by Penguin Young Readers, an imprint of Penguin Random House LLC, 345 Hudson Street, New York, New York 10014. Manufactured in China.

ISBN 9780399541421   10 9 8 7 6 5 4 3 2 1

Kate's Wish

by Lana Jacobs

Penguin Young Readers
An Imprint of Penguin Random House

Kate is having fun.

She is making silly faces

with her mom.

"I bet you can't make *this* face!"

shouts Kate.

They finish playing.

Kate looks at her mom's face.

"I wish my eyes were like yours,"

says Kate.

"They're so big and blue."

"I love your brown eyes,"

says Kate's mom.

"They're part of what makes

you special."

Kate has an idea.

She twirls with Mim-Mim

in her hands.

"Kate and Mim-Mim!

Me and you!

Let's twirl away to Mimiloo!"

In Mimiloo they see

their friend Tack.

Tack is collecting sand

for his Umbrella Flowers.

Mim-Mim wants to help!

But Mim-Mim trips,

and all the sand piles are gone.

He is sad.

He feels clumsy.

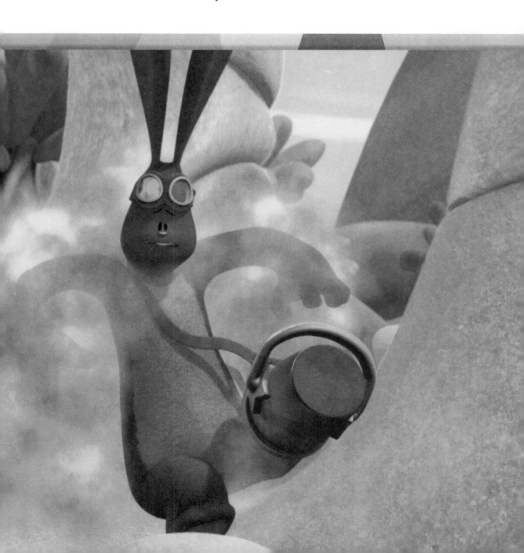

"I wish there was a way to change clumsy old me

into not-so-clumsy old me," Mim-Mim says.

Suddenly, something bumps

Mim-Mim on the head.

It is a genie's lamp!

Mim-Mim gets three wishes

from the Teenie Genie.

"I wish I wasn't clumsy anymore!"

he shouts.

The Teenie Genie snaps

his fingers.

Now Mim-Mim is riding
a unicycle while juggling!
"The clumsy old me could never
juggle like this!" he says.
Mim-Mim is excited.

Mim-Mim shows off his new skills.

He helps dig holes

for the Umbrella Flowers.

"I knew you could do it!"

Kate says.

Mim-Mim feels proud.

Now the friends wait for the

Umbrella Flowers to grow.

"I can help!" says Mim-Mim.

Mim-Mim makes his second wish

to make the flowers grow.

He sits on the flowers,

and they grow tall!

Everyone is impressed.

But Kate misses

the old Mim-Mim.

20

Mim-Mim holds Kate in his arms.

He sits on an Umbrella Flower,

and it shoots up to the sky!

"I think we're stuck," says Kate.

Mim-Mim knows how to fix
the problem.

He rubs his Teenie Genie
lamp again.

"I wish to be safe on the ground," says Mim-Mim.

The Teenie Genie snaps his fingers, and they are back on the ground.

The Umbrella Flowers
have grown too high.
The other plants will not grow
in their shade.

Mim-Mim reaches for his lamp.

Oh no!

He used up all three wishes.

"Even a Teenie Genie can't make

a better me," he says.

"There's no such thing as a better you," Kate says.

"We love you just the way you are."

"Even the silly, clumsy old me?" asks Mim-Mim.

"That's part of what makes you *you*," says Kate.

Kate knows what to do.

She grabs the Teenie Genie lamp.

"I wish for Mim-Mim to go back
to his clumsy, silly self," she says.

Then she wishes for the garden

to grow like normal.

With a snap and a dash

of sparkles, everything goes

back to normal.

"With my last wish—" starts Kate.

"You won't change anything

about yourself, will you?"

asks Mim-Mim.

"No, I like myself just the way

I am," she says.

She wishes for the Teenie Genie

to have a bigger lamp to live in!

Everyone is happy now.

Kate and Mim-Mim are back
in Kate's room.

"Do you still want to change
your big brown eyes?"
asks Kate's mom.

"No, brown eyes make me
special," she says.

"They sure do," says Kate's mom
as she hugs her tight.